Ollie and the Otter

A Scottish Osprey Story

Emily Dodd & Kirsteen Harris-Jones

When Ollie the osprey *finally* caught a fish, his best friend Rory cheered. When otters cheer they make a whistling sound:

WHEE-OOP! WHEE-OOP!

“Fishing is my new favourite thing!” shouted Ollie. “After flying!”

"And diving!

WHEEEEEE!

And fish are just so

YUMMY!"

RIPPLE SPLOSH!

"Hmmmm," said Rory. "Yes, there is something rather wonderful about catching a fish. It's almost as good as floating on your back and watching the world go by."

“I’ve not got time to float!” said Ollie. “Now I can catch, I need to learn to *throw*. If I throw a fish to Isla, she’ll make friends with me. That’s what ospreys do.”

Ollie tried to throw a fish to the **RIGHT,** but it went **LEFT.**
He tried to throw a fish **UP,** but it went **DOWN.**

He was just about to throw again when he spotted Isla below him. He let go of the fish and

WHOOSH...

...SPLAT! It landed on Rory's tummy.

"Sorry!" he called. "I'm having trouble with my aim!"

"I can see that!" said Rory.

“That was my one chance to make friends with Isla and now she’s gone,” groaned Ollie.

“She’ll be back,” said Rory. He stroked his whiskers. “Maybe you just need to practise throwing. I can help with that.”

Rory arranged leaves and berries to make a target for Ollie.

"Aim..." he shouted. "**FIRE!**"

WHOOSH! went the fish.

SPLASH! Ollie missed.

"But that target doesn't *look* like an osprey," said Ollie.

So Rory made an osprey out of a pine cone and feathers.

"Aim..." he shouted. "**FIRE!**"

WHOOSH! went the fish.

SPLASH! Ollie missed.

"But that pine cone wasn't *moving* like an osprey," said Ollie.

So Rory made some waterweed wings and stepped onto a seesaw branch. He whistled for his friend McAntlers.

McAntlers stamped his foot and Rory zoomed through the air. His waterweed wings whistled in the wind.

WHEEEEEEEE!

Ollie threw a fish.

WHOOOSH...

...SPLAT!

Ollie missed.

The fish landed, rather unfortunately, in McAntlers' antlers.

“I’ll never ever be good enough and Isla will never be my friend!” said Ollie.

“Maybe you’re trying too hard,” said Rory. “Why don’t you stop practising and do the things you love instead? When I do things I love I feel better, and then I get better at everything. Even the hard things.”

“I’m not good at anything,” said Ollie.

"What about flying?" asked Rory.

"Well, I do quite like flying," said Ollie. He took off and flew in big circles around the loch.

FLAP FLAP FLAP FLAP FLAP

He started to feel better.

"And diving?" shouted Rory. Ollie pulled his wings back and dropped like an arrow through the sky.

WHEEEEEEEE!

He felt much better. He noticed something shimmering below, and plunged into the freezing cold water…

...then flew back up clutching a silvery trout!

Ollie felt wonderful. He climbed so high he could see the snow-covered tops of the mountains. He heard the call of an osprey.

As the wind whipped his feathers, Ollie let go.

WHOOOOSH...

...CATCH!

It was Isla. She caught the fish and swooped up with her wings beating hard.

“Nice catch!” said Ollie.

“Nice throw!” said Isla. She flew a bit closer. “Sorry I messed it up last time,” she said.

“Really?” said Ollie. “I thought I was the one who messed it up!”

They laughed together, flying side by side.

Isla said, “I haven’t laughed this much since this morning, when I saw an otter with waterweed wings!”

They laughed again.

“That reminds me,” said Ollie. “I need to thank a friend.”

Rory was relaxing in the cool calm waters of the loch when

SPLAT!

A big fish landed on his belly.

"I see you've improved your aim!" called Rory.

"Yes," shouted Ollie. "Thank you for reminding me to do the things I love!"